Learning to Float

ALSO BY ALYSON TAIT

Prisoners of the Deep

Carrion

Shards of Other Skies: a collection of short stories

Learning to Float

Alyson Tait

Querencia Press, LLC
Chicago, Illinois

QUERENCIA PRESS

LIBRARY OF CONGRESS CATALOG-IN-PUBLICATION DATA

ISBN 979 8 9860788 8 5

www.querenciapress.com

First Published in 2022

Querencia Press, LLC
Chicago IL

Printed & Bound in the United States of America

CONTENTS

Dedication:

***

There are a lot of people that support me on my writing journey, and normally I would list them here—but to be frank, the words that formed this little thing weren't from them. They came from bitterness, anger, grief, and hurt.

So I don't thank any of them, but I do sometimes miss those I lost and the pieces of me I lost along the way.

little red balloons

***

Endless sea of days:
    Cloudy skies
        no desert sun
    Muddy ground
        no place to run
    Floating feet
        no tether to find
    No gravity
        no place to hide

Night sky full of stars:
    No moon
        nothing around to help count the days
    No warmth
        no leftover energy and nothing to say
    No anchor
        nothing to tie me down to the ground
    No sounds
        nothing to comfort, there's no one around

Puzzle pieces need put together but each one has a string
    Tied around the middle, and every time the wind picks
up
They float up
    and up and up they go
        Scattered across the air
The table's coated in glue
So it's sticky to the touch, and half the puzzle is laid
Down, grasping to the particles.

Helium fills your lungs, and when you try
To breath
      To think
            To eat
You simply float.

But when you try to lift yourself up
      Try to fly
            because gravity's become
      Too heavy
You realize, every time, that the helium
It's turned
To carbon and it sinks
      And you still
            Can't breathe.

Pretending

***

At sixteen, my best friend
pretended
to be my girlfriend
at a skating rink concert.

My leg over hers, I
pretended
to be just pretending,
when I looked into her eyes.

Later, when a boy and I kissed
I pretended
to be deeply shocked,
instead of hungry for more.

I spent that whole night
pretending that
I wasn't confused. Instead, I was
dramatic because we were sixteen.

Years later—it occurred to me.
So many things occur to me
now that I've stopped
pretending.

Discovering the first stage of grief

***

I remember the night; I was about to join a voice-chat, then Facebook messenger dinged.

Instead, I avoided the event for months because the casual news of your suicide haunted my thoughts.

Weren't social events more your style anyway? Weren't you the friend always dragging me to parties?

You tried, anyway.

For days I hunted for the good news that the bad news was fake, waiting for you to reappear, and searching for an obituary that never came.

Without closure came a strange, tainted distance. I recovered well enough, I guess.

But voice-chats feel a bit stranger than they used to.

A little bit

***

Twelve white bobbles, grown from scratch

Wilted mistletoe and twigs of baby's breath

Whispered chants and sickly

Sweet incense fill the air

The fairie circle shimmers in the moonlight

As I sit somewhere in the middle of the ring

Wondering about you

And your hallucinations

The bobbles go down one by one, chewed—

then spit back into the grass that grew them

They taste like you. You both leave me

Empty. Leave me to wither unsatiated.

Like Mushrooms

***

The witch withers without her wand.

She struggles to justify the rotting regents on her blessed

racks,

or the faded moments she spends searching the forest.

No one understands why she wastes the day—

or why she feels so empty all the time.

Without her wand, she's not herself.

It's the one thing she controls.

The treadmill takes me through my forest.

Halogen lights make morning fog.

The spices on my kitchen counter expired three years ago,

but it's harder to justify an empty fridge

when other people visit and leer around my life

Without counting, I'm not myself.

It's the one thing I control.

The witch and I have much in common:

Making spells and creating illusions, avoiding judgment.

We duck and dodge at the rattle of other humans,

And live in the comfort of darkness

But at least we have control.

In the Forest

***

Orange-red flames consumed the summer.

Its ash marked a starting line behind the trees.

Hot, messy, and tempting.

The feeling was familiar.

Smoke clings to leaves, bark, and moss

Jumping to visitors, attaching itself

To curly hair and cotton sundresses

No discrimination between living

And dead.

Just like darkness, or moonlight

Which is all that remains of that summer

Now that the fire you started is gone.

And the moon doesn't fill the gaps in your teeth

But sometimes it carries your voice.

Smoke clings to that, too.

Welcome to high-school friendships

Where all the expenses and bruises are
Forgiven because memories are
Priceless

1 message from a mutual friend:
(To inform me that you'd passed)

$0.00

1 message from a closer mutual friend:
(To inform me that you'd passed)

$0.00

6 friend requests from old mutual friends
(Because death brings everyone closer)

$0.00

1 night spent lying awake in bed
(Wondering when you'd declare the joke is dead)

$0.00

1 TV show finale bonded to your memory
(Would I have always cried when Q said goodbye?)
$0.00

3 months spent barely writing
(All I could think about was all the days I didn't message you)
$0.00

1 informal memorial service
(That I couldn't attend from across the country)
$0.00

Bulk

Hours spent disassociating
(Hoping in vain it would take away the sadness)
$0.00

Revelations about my other best friends
(I always thought grief was fairly universal)
$0.00

Total:

$You're still gone.

Thank you for shopping with us today.

The cost of your life Priceless. No dollar bills to assign the laughs and tears you gave to the world in life, and death, but it's disingenuous to say that it didn't have a cost, my dear old friend—my dear nostalgic parents and aunts of yesteryear. Your absence is felt and it is costly and I'll never feel quite okay, so here is my receipt for you to someday—across the veil and in another life, to repay the costless debt you've marked down here on earth.

Terms and conditions apply*

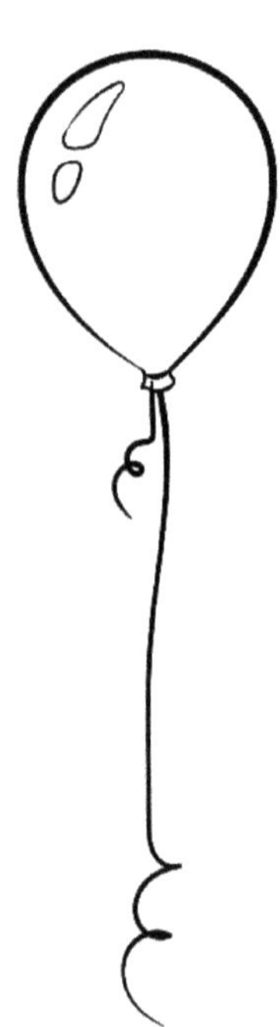

espial

***

It's the moment her hips tilt
and hot breaths of air fill the room
that my consciousness wilts
and coherent thoughts evaporate directly off my skin.

Affirmations never served in war
and their front line exists mostly in mirrored rooms
But that confirmation *is* the bar
and lifted up, it shows who I was waiting to become

Yet eventually the sheets turn cold again,
and the door itself is melancholy
having let the winter air back in
and the parts of me that ache are different than they were
before.

Empty Cogitation

***

heart pounds rapidly against your chest as your
stomach slides beneath my
shaking hands
and my mouth waters but im
empty and void of thoughts

heart aches as i stare at the door you left through
stomach grumbles but i cant find the will to feed it
when my hands are clawing at the inside of my pockets
my mouth whimpers
and the room feels empty

heart weakens
stomach growls louder
hands refuse to reach for food and
my mouth has ceased to talk about it
the voices remind me that im just not empty enough quite
yet

Tumbleweeds

***

Tumbleweeds roll across the thirsty, cracking ground.

The spindles itch and scratch the neglected surface of the earth.

Like I imagined your fingernails would feel along my back.

Your kiss was an event—

A year of looking to the horizon and longing

Like the cactus and her flowers watch

For the monsoons to roll over the mountains

—your lips on my skin

The sky disappears and everything

Floods.

The dips and valleys all fill

In a way nothing else achieves.

Maladaptive Reverie

***

i close my eyes and astral project a piece of me
she's pale and free
her feet float just above the ground
not *quite* walking around
because my chains don't paralyze or tether her
they just don't transfer

the coolness of my pillow becomes your skin
my indulgence. my sin
your face is flawless. pale. immortal.
heavenly—ok. normal. sort of.
hazel eyes lap up her features and for a moment, you two match,
an itch i could never scratch

i can only lie, staring up at the popcorn ceiling, and watch the movie play
paralyzed while my ghost's away
she's gotten brave, ventured further each time i let her out
seeking you without a doubt
she's begun to leave little pieces out there behind her,

pieces of me. little brutal reminders.

reminding me that our lips won't meet because i can't
control the past, or present, or future. i can't strip the color
from my world to greet you, statuesque with satin lips. i can
only daydream and try to slow down my fate.

so i astral project, again, and try to control
my slow demise

Rusted Shut

***

We three fit together like a chain link fence for a while.

Locked in place and indestructible.

But when we overgrew on just one side, (she) walked away.

Her link rusted, and some little piece of me corroded, stuck to
you.

She healed and survived for a while.

I wilted. Slowly all the links rusted. They faded away, lost in
the winter wind.

Crumbled by the summer sun.

I lost my grip and floated away, and watched her settle in.

I clawed towards (her), desperate to

Heal.

But you stayed—

home.

And I stayed—

adrift.

And she stayed—

gone.

And eating crumpets, too.

***

Showing ankles like a Victorian working-class lady, and it's fine, but I giggle when I think about you, and I wish I could be right there by your side.

Grazing my fingertips across your neck and losing my breath every time you move your lips—everything just feels right.

But it has to be clothes and we can't be close and I just wanna open my door, but I can't even tell anyone about it—all so asinine.

Hair falling in your face. Mine, yours, ours, and then I wake you from this dream. Honestly, it's always been the very hardest late at night.

Needless to say, I'm odds and ends

***

nightly routine:
stars come out / energy fades
brain winds down / thoughts land in a gutter
lights go out.
chiming fills my ears forever / because despite everything
she still has to answer the call.

she usually does

i watch her through a screen.
webcam shows every imperfection.
gone are the days of usb-port orbs you straddle
on your monitor;
no.
her laptop shows high definition.
it connects the two of us as if we were in the same room.
i soak up every luscious curve and soft-edged freckle.
even the conversation she's having—
reflected in her glasses.

her love is fleeting.
impersonal. ill tempered. far sighted and white hot like a
burning star
just like her.
they're both spoiled.

in reality: i was the spoiled one.
fawned over / praised / eaten up by her honey-colored
eyes and red lips
then i spoiled
watching her.

i went rotten in and out
silently with shallow breaths and a green fire in my belly.

the sickly beast corroded.
it hollowed me out
made me crave more until i absorbed her.
i absorbed her and lost myself.

i ate up and tried to become my best friend, my lover, my
queen.

but in the silence behind the hum of my computer, i
wonder.
did she forget me?
did her consciousness slip so far
that she forgot there was someone watching her?
spending time with her?
i almost ask. then she turns to me and my voice box melts.

maybe i'll take the risk tomorrow.
but maybe the star and it's white-hot heat will finally
explode
and i won't have to ask at all.

Tiptoe.

***

A lifetime ago, before the earth tiptoed around the sun, I sat by the fire with a book in my hands. It was a book about oceans, salt, and old gods reaching their hands into the new world. It was the first big rainstorm of the season, and even with my vodka, blanket, music, and alternate reality, I couldn't get warm enough to ignore the sounds.

A different age, in another place, I wouldn't have wanted to. I would have sat on the porch with whoever I could drag, and we would reach out our hands—grabbing at the torrents until the desert ground drank it up away from us. I would throw my blanket to the ground and dance until it soaked my bones, and I'd have to shower just to shave it all away from my skin. Back when I passed by cactuses on my way to the corner store, I'd beg for rain and thunder. The sound is different by the fire, near the water, and far away from it all.

Rain becomes nostalgia.

Loneliness and memories.

The way it slaps against the cement and crawls / down /

the / windows / is

Pure anxiety.

A crash of thunder puts the fear of God into my belly. That

part isn't new. I recognize that as my face scrunches at my

straw. My fingers send a message, and then I pull the book back

up to my face, trying to concentrate on descriptions of gowns

made for grieving princesses. I'm really just listening for the

notification.

I'm thinking about monsoons in July.

I'm picturing the T.V. reflected in her eyes.

I'm shuddering at the thought of the next boom of thunder

and as lightning strikes somewhere past my window—

I flinch.

Body jumps

and my book drops on my cup when my phone sings.

It was an old god reaching into my world to tell me

The rain is just in my head.

The rain is just a

Simile / metaphor / tactile representation of

The things I never say out loud.

Even when the rain is actually a downpour, washing away

the chalk on my front steps.

It took a dozen paper towels to clean up the mess, and by

the time I finished, I couldn't even pretend to focus on the

words. The pages were soggy, and I scolded myself. So I put

the book away and thought about crawling into bed. The

forecast had a clear sky the next day, and maybe waking up to a

blinding sun was what I'd needed.

Maybe it too would remind me of the desert.

I can't stand graveyards, so I do the next best thing.

***

Fertilized soil lives beyond my front door.
Perfect squares nestled around brass sprinklers.
Thin dirt footpaths chiseled between plowed rows,
so heavy feet never have to trample the barren soil.

The whole thing is a mirage.

It's a manufactured trick of the eyes.
A planned deception at a cellular level.
I purchase seeds daily at the general store,
and toss them in a moldy box when I get home.

The whole thing is a ploy.

You live behind the general store.
Brightly colored blue hair frames your face.
An amused grin that feels impossible to ignore.
I came back the next day. And then again the next.

The whole thing got away from me.

My heart beats rapidly in my chest.
Heavy knots form deep in my stomach.
Words keep getting stuck inside my throat,
making it difficult to actually try and flirt with you

The whole thing is insecurity.

Off I go, today,
to buy more seeds,
in the hope I'll see you
as you make your way into town.

Acknowledgments

***

A Little Bit, Like Mushrooms, and In the Forest will appear in Deitrich in May 2022

Total price of your death appeared in HAD in January, 2022

Tiptoe appeared in Anser Journal in 2021

Needless to say, I'm odds and ends appeared in neurological literary magazine in April 2021

Rusted Shut will appear in Pink Plastic House in May 2022

About the Author:

***

Alyson lives in Maryland where she got married, had her daughter, and began her writing journey. She has appeared in (mac)ro(mic), Wrongdoing Magazine,Twin Pies Lit, and Pyre Magazine,and HAD—among others. You can find her on Amazon, and Twitter @rudexvirus1. Her website is AlysonTait.com. Alyson also helps run Inkfort Press.